We're Taking An Airplane Trip

By DINAH L. MOCHÉ

Illustrated by

CAROLYN BRACKEN

The author wishes to thank Gordon S. Williams at the Boeing Company and the following people at Trans World Airlines, Inc.: Angus McClure, Joyce Bennis, Marcia Lawrence, and Sally C. McElwreath.

A GOLDEN BOOK, New York
Western Publishing Company, Inc.
Racine, Wisconsin 53404

"We're here! We're here!" Elizabeth said happily as the taxi stopped at the airplane terminal. Elizabeth and Jimmy Baldwin were going to visit their grandparents. It was their first airplane trip, and they were flying by themselves.

"Mr. Bear is a little scared,"
said Jimmy, hugging his teddy bear.
"But I'm going to hold him the whole way."
"Mr. Bear has nothing to worry about,"
said Mrs. Baldwin. "Airplane trips
are exciting."

"Mommy, may we sit by a window?"
Elizabeth asked when they reached the
check-in counter.

The ticket agent smiled. "Let me check my
computer," he said. He pressed some buttons and
looked at the screen. "Yes," he said, "I have just the
seats for you." Then he gave them special flight pins
to wear.

The agent put flight tags on the suitcases and set them on a conveyor belt. Away they went, through a door in the wall. "Where is my suitcase going?" asked Jimmy.

"Down to the baggage handlers," said his mother. "They will put it on the plane."

The ticket agent gave Mrs. Baldwin boarding passes and told her that the children's plane would be leaving from Gate 9. On the way the Baldwins saw all kinds of stores and restaurants full of people. Jimmy liked the busy terminal, but he held on tightly to his mother's hand—and Mr. Bear, too.

They stopped at the security area, where security agents were making sure that no one carried anything dangerous onto the plane.

Elizabeth and her mother put their bags on the conveyor belt to be checked by the x-ray machine. Then they all walked through the metal detector.

cargo train

maintenance

baggage train

While they waited in the departure lounge, Elizabeth and Jimmy looked out the big windows and saw their jumbo jet. Mechanics were checking the engines. Fuel was being pumped into tanks in the wings. Baggage and supplies were being loaded on board.

water truck

fuel truck

COMMISSARY SERVICE

mail truck

Finally it was time for Elizabeth and Jimmy to board the plane. They went with their mother ahead of the other passengers.

A flight attendant named Becky showed Elizabeth and Jimmy where their seats were. "I will take good care of the children," Becky told Mrs. Baldwin.

Mrs. Baldwin kissed Jimmy and Elizabeth. "I have to go now," she said. "I'll call you tonight. Have fun."

Jimmy looked worried, but Becky told him she had a special treat for them.

Soon all the passengers were in their seats.
The flight attendants stood in the aisles to
show them how to use the safety equipment.
Jimmy was looking out the window.

"Jimmy," Elizabeth whispered, "you're
supposed to watch."

High up in the airport control tower, the air traffic controllers watched as Elizabeth and Jimmy's plane moved away from the terminal, then turned and taxied slowly to the runway.

One controller talked to the pilot by radio, telling him that there were four planes on the runway ahead of the jumbo jet.

Finally the controller told the pilot that he was clear for takeoff. The engines on the big jet began to roar.

The plane raced down the runway, faster and faster. Elizabeth and Jimmy felt as if they were being pushed back against their seats. Then the plane lifted off the ground and began to climb into the air. Elizabeth's ears felt stopped up. She swallowed and yawned to make them feel better.

The plane climbed higher. The houses and cars down below looked like toys.

Then the plane went above the clouds and the sunny sky looked very clear.

Jimmy unbuckled his seat belt when the sign went off and walked down the aisle to the bathroom.

As Jimmy closed the bathroom door, the lights went on by themselves. Jimmy looked at everything in the bathroom. The little bars of soap on the sink were just the right size for Mr. Bear.

Elizabeth lowered the tray attached to the seat in front of her. It was like a little table to put things on.

Before dinner, Elizabeth
and Jimmy switched seats.
Becky gave them each a
dinner tray. "Mr. Bear
is going to eat his chocolate
cake first," said Jimmy.

Later the flight attendants
turned down the lights to show
a movie. Elizabeth put on
earphones so she could hear
the movie. Jimmy fell asleep.

Soon after the movie the pilot announced that the plane was about to land. Jimmy woke up and stretched, and he and Elizabeth made sure their seat belts were fastened. It was dark outside now. They could see the airport lights shining below as the plane went down, down, down. Suddenly there was a bump as the wheels touched the runway. The plane slowed down and taxied to the terminal.

Becky took Elizabeth and Jimmy through the jetway to the terminal. Grandma and Grandpa Baldwin were waiting for them. Elizabeth and Jimmy hugged Becky, then ran to their grandparents.

While they waited for their suitcases in the baggage claim area, Jimmy told his grandparents all about the flight. "Mr. Bear thought it was fun," he said. "He wasn't even scared—because I held him the whole way."